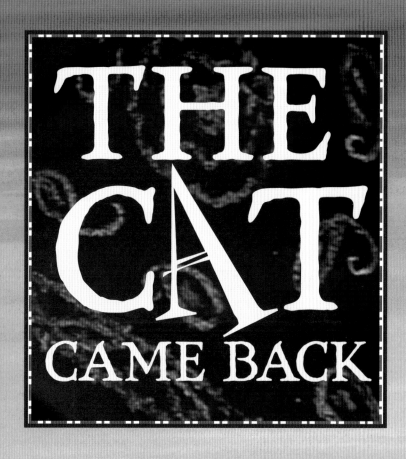

THE CAT CAME BACK

FRED PENNER

ILLUSTRATED BY RENÉE REICHERT

A NEAL PORTER BOOK
ROARING BROOK PRESS
NEW MILFORD, CONNECTICUT

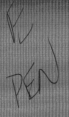

Text copyright © 2005 by Fred Penner

Illustrations copyright © 2005 by Renée Reichert

A Neal Porter Book

Published by Roaring Brook Press

Roaring Brook Press is a division of Holtzbrinck Publishing Holdings Limited Partnership

143 West Street, New Milford, Connecticut 06776

Distributed in Canada by H. B. Fenn and Company Ltd.

Library of Congress Cataloging-in-Publication Data

Penner, Fred.

The cat came back / by Fred Penner ; illustrated by Renée Reichert.— 1st ed.

p. cm.

"A Neal Porter book."

Summary: A persistent and indestructible cat keeps coming back, despite his owner's attempts to give him away.

ISBN 1-59643-030-3

1. Folk songs, English—United States—Texts.   [1. Cats—Songs and music.   2. Folk songs—United States.]   I. Reichert, Renée, ill.   II. Title.

PZ8.3.P385Cat 2005

782.42162'13'00268--dc22

2004019980

Roaring Brook Press books are available for special promotions and premiums.

For details contact: Director of Special Markets, Holtzbrinck Publishers.

First edition September 2005

Book design by Jennifer Browne

Printed in the United States of America

2 4 6 8 10 9 7 5 3 1

Nothing is more important than the unity and strength of the Family.
I dedicate this book to my Family, my wife Odette and our children,
Damien, Hayley, Danica and Kendra.
Read to your children.
—F. P.

To Bill
—R. R.

A cat saw some milk as he watched from a tree.
"That old snoring man must have meant it for me."
Then an interesting thought leapt into his mind.
"This might be the home I've been hoping to find."

From the tree

To the porch

To the feast on the floor

He awoke Mr. Johnson at the end of a snore.
Johnson let the cat finish for the cat was kind of cute.
Then he showed the cat the road and gave the cat the boot.

And the cat came back the very next day.
The cat came back—we thought he was a goner.
But the cat came back.
He just couldn't stay away.

The cat moved in with the man, fish and birds.
But old Mr. Johnson thought this was quite absurd.
So he labored day and night to build the cat a house
With lots of pillows, some catnip and a little rubber mouse.

But the cat came back the very next day.
The cat came back—we thought he was a goner.
But the cat came back.
He just couldn't stay away.

This man was not the type to bicker or complain.
He knew what he must do—something most humane.
The society came 'round with a cat cage and a truck.
Little did he know that his plan would run amuck.

For the cat came back the very next day.
The cat came back—we thought he was a goner.
But the cat came back.
He just couldn't stay away.

A big old pirate
     put the cat into a box
And wrapped up
     the pirate chest
With pirate chains
     and pirate locks.

Off the cliff,

Down, down, down

Deep into the sea.

"Hooray!" cried Mr. Johnson. "At last I am free!"

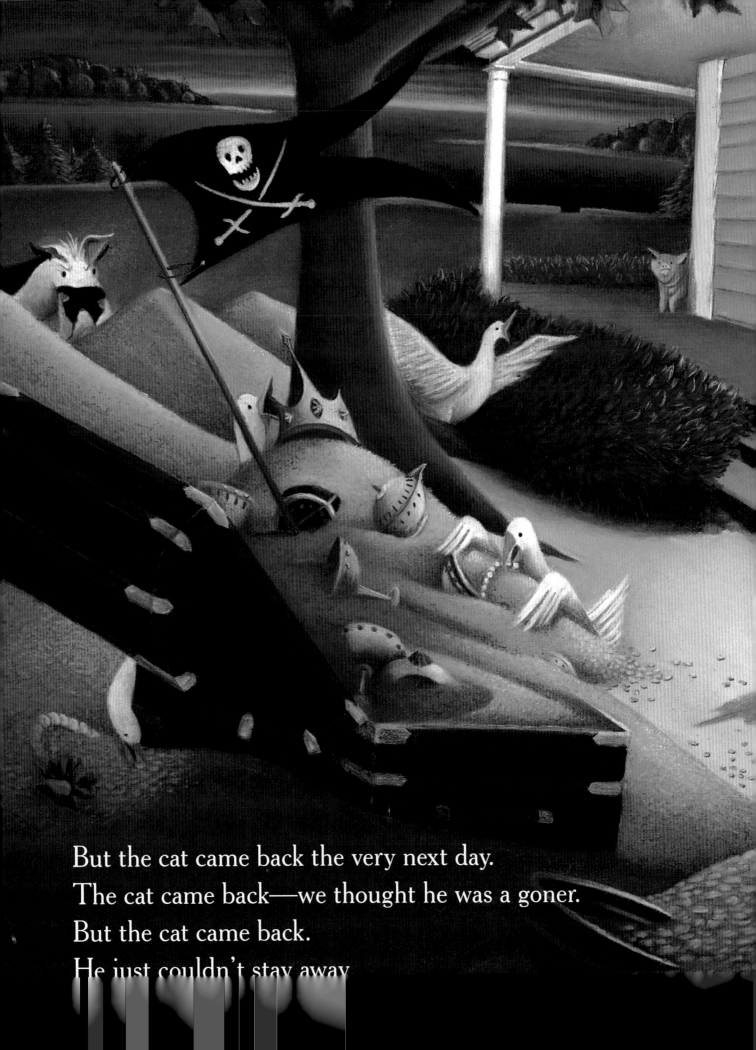

But the cat came back the very next day.
The cat came back—we thought he was a goner.
But the cat came back.
He just couldn't stay away.

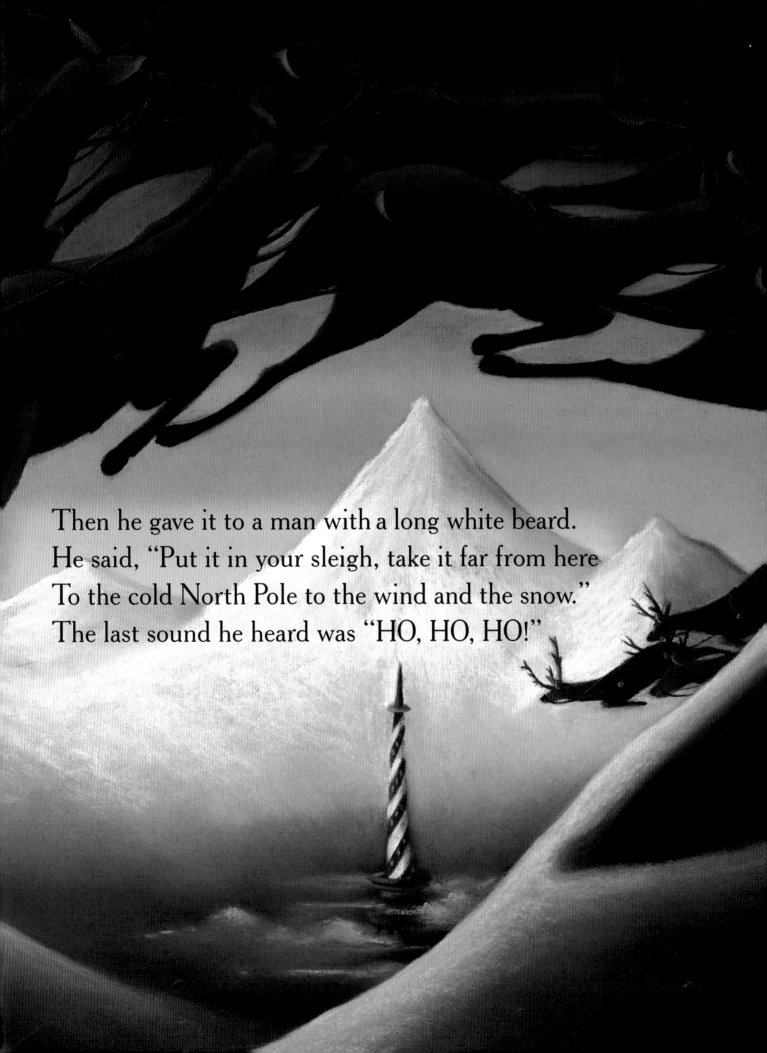

Then he gave it to a man with a long white beard.
He said, "Put it in your sleigh, take it far from here
To the cold North Pole to the wind and the snow."
The last sound he heard was "HO, HO, HO!"

But the cat came back
the very next day.
The cat came back—
we thought he was a goner.
But the cat came back.
He just couldn't stay away.

LOVE
SANTA

Straight up! Where no cat's gone before
Toward the twinkling stars
Aboard a homemade rocketship bound for Planet Mars.

He crashed into an asteroid with a meow and a ROAR!
That cat was surely gone for good . . . lost forever more.

But the cat came back the very next day.
The cat came back—we thought he was a goner.
The cat came back . . .

He just couldn't stay away!